Every Pony

Has a Tale

This book is dedicated to

Edward H. and Ann Allen
&
Don Wegner

whose generous donations financed the publication of this book.

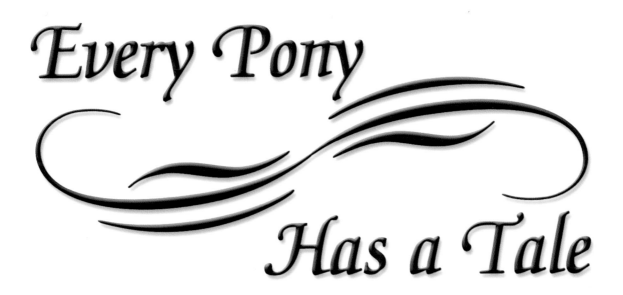

Every Pony Has a Tale

by

CAROUSEL STORYTELLERS, INK

Published by
Beautiful America Publishing Company
P.O. Box 244
Woodburn, OR 97071

Library of Congress Cataloging-in-Publication Data
Library of Congress Catalog Number 2003011051

ISBN 0-89802-787-X

Printed in Korea

Table of Contents

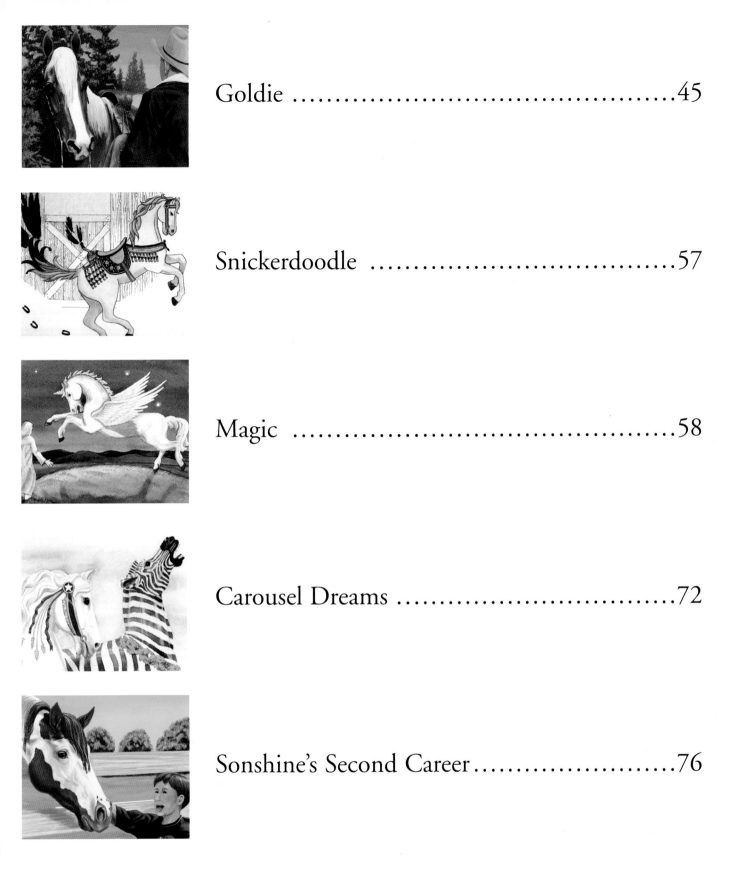

Introduction

*T*his book is for people who believe in magic. It's also for those who *think* they believe in magic. Of course, the *rest* of you are welcome to read it, too. But be forewarned–the chances are quite good that you will *become* believers by the time you read the final word.

Here's how the magic works:

As you read, you hold the page just so, and faint images begin to appear – rather like a photograph slowly developing in a darkroom. Silky horses' tails seem to flick across the page, and at times, you could swear you just heard a pony nicker softly in your ear. You may feel warm breath tickling the back of your neck as you turn each page. Suddenly, you are humming the familiar melodies of the Carousel's band organ, and you imagine you are in another space and time. If any of these things happen as you read this book, then the magic has started its work on you. It may take awhile to become aware of the magic – so just read on.

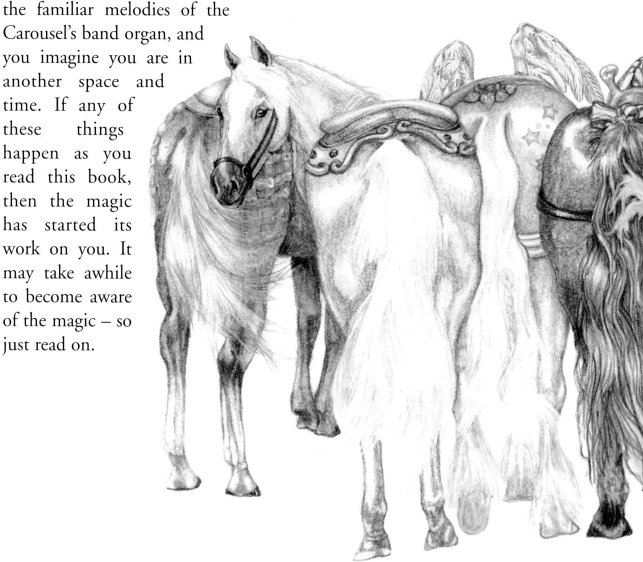

There is something here for everyone, no matter whether you're a boy or girl, whether you're 8 years old or 80. Between these colorful covers are stories, poems, and artistic delights that are sure to make you smile or sniffle, and maybe even *think* or *remember*. At the very least, you will be touched by the magic that is synonymous with the word – CAROUSEL!

The fun of collecting the entries for this book has been as magical as the creation of the Carousel itself. At the beginning of the Carousel project, a diverse group of people came together with the goal of building a hand-carved carousel, a community legacy for children of all ages. And so it was with the Carousel Storytellers group. Public response to our children's books has been so positive that we decided to write a book containing a variety of stories and artwork, all in one publication.

It's a tribute to the uniqueness of the individuals and how they came together to produce a work of art. Our goal was simple: Give our readers a feast for the eyes and ears, mind and heart.

Enjoy the magic.
— *Chris Patterson*

Front cover, pages 6-7 and rear cover illustrations by Cheryl Degner

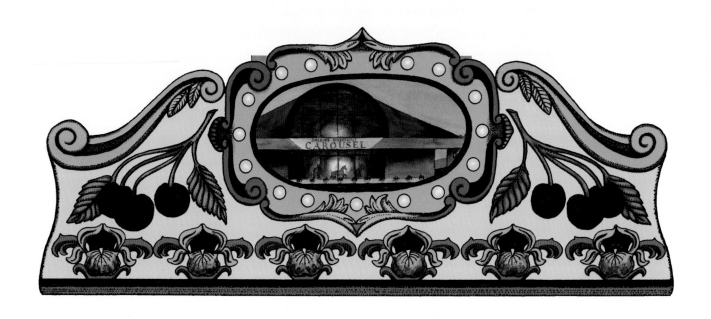

Grace and Richard

Written by
Christina Patterson

Illustrated by
Kathy Haney

Grace and Richard

Grace and Richard came to play
At the Carousel one day.
They decided they would stay
All morning long.

Up and Down and 'round they flew;
Every horse's name they knew;
Riding on the wagons, too,
All day long.

Evening came to end the ride;
Grace and Richard ran to hide;
Snuggled up to Stardust's side
All night long.

Morning came and morning went.
Soon their tokens all were spent.
Grace and Richard never meant
To stay so long!

The weeks flew past; they couldn't bear
To leave their precious ponies there
And so they stayed — that silly pair —
All month long.

Time moved on and there they were,
In summer shorts and winter fur.
She loved him and he loved her,
All year long.

If you were in the park last night,
You might have seen some candlelight
In the windows, burning bright--
All night long.

On Grace's birthday cake, I hear,
Were ninety candles—one per year.
Richard said, "We'll stay right here
Our whole life long!"

As Grace and Richard's life will tell,
Everyone's young on a carousel!
So live each moment, live it well
Your whole life long.

SALEM'S RIVERFRONT CAROUSEL

Hero's Wish

Written and Illustrated by
Janee Hughes

*T*he little bay colt frisked around the pasture with the other young horses, growing strong and healthy in the spring sunshine. He was smaller than the draft horse colts, but quick and agile. His watchful mother let her spunky baby know that he was special. His father, she told him, was not a draft horse, but a very refined and handsome saddle horse. She knew that her son could excel at anything.

As the first three years of his life passed, the young colt spent more and more time with the people on the farm, especially the owner, Henry. Henry was kind and patient as he taught the young horses to lead, drive, and pull farm implements. Henry called the bay colt "the little guy" because he wasn't as big as the other horses. The little colt felt he had to try harder to keep up with the bigger horses. He learned quickly, and always gave his best effort, earning Henry's affection and trust.

The little guy worked in the fields along with the other horses. He had to work hard to pull his share of the load, but he enjoyed being useful. When the work was done, there was always a clean, warm stall and plenty of sweet-smelling hay. Some days he didn't have to work, but just enjoyed the company of the other horses in the pasture. It was a good life.

But what the little horse enjoyed most were the children. Often they arrived at the barn near the end of the day as the horses were coming in from their work. The barn came alive to their laughter and screams of delight. The smallest ones were placed gently on the little

guy's back so he could carry them around the pasture. He was very, very careful. It was soon apparent that he could be trusted to take care of them. The children loved him.

One afternoon, as the children came running gleefully down the barn aisle, the youngest little girl, Ann, cried, "There's my Hero!"

The other children laughed at her. "Your hero! Horses can't be heroes, silly. 'My Hero'!" But silly as it was, the name stuck. Henry heard it and knew it fit perfectly.

The years passed, the children grew up, and Hero worked contentedly on the farm. There were fewer horses now, with more work being done by tractors. There was still enough work for Hero, who could be ridden or driven, and Henry used him mostly for light work. But Hero missed the company of the other horses. Even more, he missed the children.

One morning Hero got a very special treat. Henry loaded him into a trailer and said, "We've got a big job to do today, old fella. I hope you're up to it." When the truck came to a stop, Hero found himself in a very pretty park near the river. Some trees were being thinned, and Hero was to pull them out from among the standing trees. Henry harnessed him and led him across the park.

Hero noticed a large building, and some men were opening huge doors on the side facing him. As he drew closer, he saw a round platform, and on it were brightly colored figures of horses in lively poses. But they were not at all like the horses he knew—no, these were incredibly

beautiful horses! Each one was proudly prancing, and each had marvelous, brightly colored trappings, braids, ribbons, and jewels! He had never seen anything like it!

They continued on their way, and Hero went to work pulling logs. It was tricky work, straining his muscles as he carefully followed Henry's commands to make sharp turns and quick stops. They finished the job without damaging any of the standing trees, and Hero felt proud of his skill.

Tired and dirty, Hero followed Henry back across the park. Eagerly, he looked for the Carousel, and to his surprise, saw that the magnificent horses were now charging around the platform, moving up and down, up and down. There were bright lights, mirrors and music. And all of the horses were carrying children! How wonderful! Oh, how he wished he could jump on that platform and become one of those horses!

He looked back over his shoulder as he was led away, storing the magical scene in his memory.

More years passed, and Hero grew old and stiff. Henry was very good to him, and didn't ask him to work any more. Hero spent most of his time feeling a little bored as he stood in the shade of a tree or dozed in his stall. He often thought of that wonderful day when he saw the Carousel, but he never got a chance to go back and see it again.

Hero led a long, productive life, but one night, as he lay sleeping in the deep straw of his stall, his spirit peacefully left this world.

The end of Hero's life was also the end of an era. Tractors now do the farm work, but they cannot replace the friendship and dedication of the wonderful old draft horses. Henry's granddaughter, Ann, has not forgotten her grandfather's farm and the steady, dependable horses. So when Salem began building a carousel, she knew that it had to include a draft horse—her Hero.

When you visit the carousel in Salem's Riverfront Park, look for our little Hero, his bay coat shining, his neck proudly arched, colorful ribbons braided into his mane. He is making wishes come true for the children, as he always loved to do!

The End

A Job
For Justice

Written by
Nancy M. Hadley

Illustrated by
Kathleen S. Hoth

I had to get going! There was no time to lose!
I'd just heard some wonderful, marvelous news!
When a friend of mine casually made the remark
That a carousel opened at Riverfront Park!

I knew he was right (he had very good sources),
As sure as I felt they'd need carousel horses!
So excited and eager to go and apply,
I had hopes they'd be willing to give me a try.

I knew there'd be those who consider me small,
But I'd work really hard and I'd always stand tall!
So I hopped on a Cherriot bus for the park,
On a quest for adventure about to embark!

I practically flew through the carousel door,
But had no idea what was waiting in store!
For there on the platform, all shiny and new,
Were beautiful horses, in bright colored hues.

Once upon
a time a
castle high
a hill lived

K.S. Hath

The wagons and horses were all in their places,

It didn't appear there were *any* more spaces.

Then someone said they even had *spares,*

To fill in when some of them needed repairs.

The largest horse spoke as he flashed me a grin.

"Son, if we *had* room, you would never fit in!

You're made of metal — we're wood, painted bright!

And you're way too little — it wouldn't be right!"

I knew it was true and I hung my head low,

And turning around, I decided to go.

I had hoped to be part of this carousel team,

But guess that was just a small horse's big dream.

I jumped when I heard someone calling my name,

"Hey, Justice, we really are glad that you came!

There's a '*high-up*' position that we have to fill,

If you're okay with heights, you might fit the bill!"

Afraid of high places? I had no such fear,

It appeared there might be a spot for me here!

At the peak of the carousel roof it was planned,

A golden horse weather vane would proudly stand!

It *was* pretty high, though I didn't care.
I'd be part of the carousel and thrilled to be there!
The man climbed the ladder that led to the roof,
And I carefully followed him, hoof after hoof.

When we got to the top, I jumped right on the pole,
For I knew I was destined for this lofty role!
I held my head high, standing upright and bold,
As they started to paint my new coating of gold.

Now I'm on duty each day and each night,
And watch o'er the river as herons take flight.
And my 'gold leaf' heart always puffs up with pride,
When the children come for their carousel ride.

So be sure to gaze skyward when you come to play,
And give me a wave or a smile on your way.
For no matter the weather, in gray skies or blue,
I'll always be there, looking out over you!

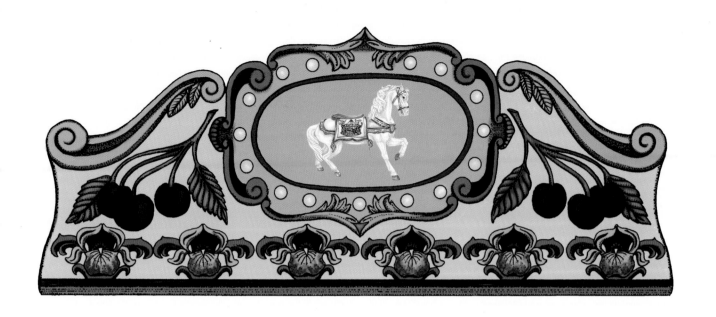

Cutting Ambassador Down To Size

Written by
Elaine Sanchez

Illustrated by
Cheryl Degner

Everyone thought Ambassador was going to be the perfect horse to represent Salem's Riverfront Carousel. He was the last horse to be carved, and the only one to have fancy designs on both sides. That alone made him special.

Dave, the head carver, had created a likeness of the entire Carousel on Ambassador's right side, including horses, shields, ribbons, and hundreds of tiny twinkling lights. And on the left side, he'd carved

knives, mallets and brushes to represent the tools used by all the artists who helped build the Carousel.

It had taken months to carve Ambassador, and the day the work was finally finished Dave proudly put the horse on display. Dozens of people came to admire Ambassador, and they all squeezed in close, trying to pet his face or touch his intricate carvings.

And as closely as everyone looked, no one noticed that there was something very wrong with Ambassador. It wasn't in the design or the carving. It was just one of those odd quirks of nature that no one could have predicted.

Somehow a large wad of sawdust had gotten stuck between Ambassador's ears and his brain. It had been there from the very beginning, making it impossible for him to hear a single sound. And since he couldn't hear, he didn't understand his job. And that's the reason everything got so messed up.

It was too bad that on Ambassador's first day of meeting the public, a rather large woman got bumped from behind and lost her balance. Trying to steady herself, she reached out for Ambassador's neck. But instead of grabbing him, she accidentally *pushed* him. And THUNK!

It happened that quickly.
Poor Ambassador fell.
His chin hit the floor
HARD, and everyone
gasped at the sound of
splintering wood.

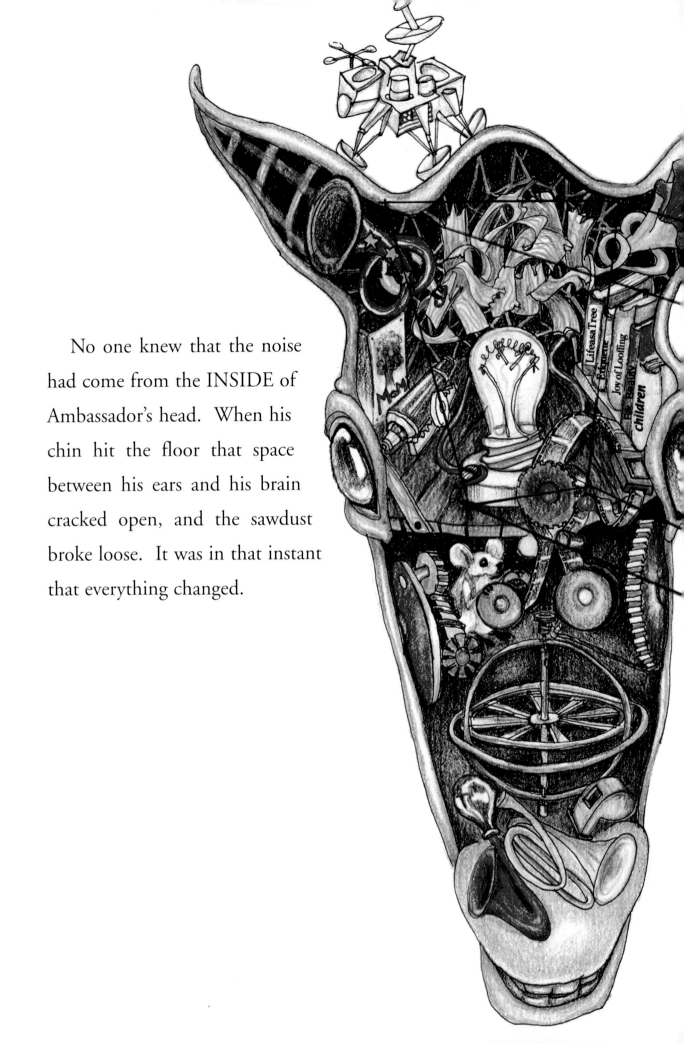

No one knew that the noise had come from the INSIDE of Ambassador's head. When his chin hit the floor that space between his ears and his brain cracked open, and the sawdust broke loose. It was in that instant that everything changed.

Ambassador could hear!

He awoke with a jolt. He heard voices crying out, "NO! NO! OH, NO!"

"Poor Ambassador!"

"Is he hurt?"

"Is anything broken?"

"Will he be all right?"

"Can he be fixed?"

Ambassador felt warm hands lifting him up.

They must be talking about me, he thought.

Someone said, "His ears are still on."

And somebody else said, "That's good!"

"And his tail isn't broken."

"What a relief!"

"His legs look okay."

"Wonderful!"

"None of his teeth are chipped."

And then someone said, "Uh-oh. He's got a really nasty scrape on his chin."

A big man took Ambassador's head in his rough hands and examined the wound. "We can fix that with some sandpaper."

"Whew! What a relief! It looks like our beautiful boy is going to be just fine."

"Thank goodness! Can you imagine how disappointed everyone would be if something bad happened to Ambassador?"

"It would be awful. So many hearts would be broken. People all over the state are waiting for him to visit. He's a very important horse, and everyone loves him."

"You got that right."

Ambassador felt dizzy and confused, like he'd been asleep for months — years, maybe. He thought he could remember being tall, and he could *almost* picture a soft green forest in his mind, but who could concentrate with all of these people talking at the same time?

Why were they saying he was beautiful? And special? And loved? Why would he be?

He remained very still while a woman with a kind voice rubbed his chin with something rough and said, "Don't you worry, Ambassador. We'll get those scratches sanded out and you'll be good as new in no time. You're way too important to go around looking bunged up."

I'm important? He wasn't exactly sure what that meant, but he liked the way it sounded. The longer he listened to people talk, the more impressed he became with himself. They called him *special, glorious,* and *splendid.* They talked about the places he'd go. Soon he'd be traveling to the state capitol, to schools and universities. He'd be the guest of honor at big parties and the marshal of grand parades.

I really am something special! he thought.

The next morning Dave brought Sandy, the head painter, into the carving studio. Sandy hummed softly while she pulled out some tubes of paint and a few brushes. Ambassador liked the gentle sounds she made.

She ran her hand over his back and said, "How's our beautiful Ambassador horse this morning?"

Sandy circled around Ambassador checking the wooden skin on his back and belly, tail and mane. "I don't want my paint to be lumpy, Ambassador. So I have to make sure you don't have any nicks or bumps."

She took his face in both of her hands, then tilting her head first one way, then the other, she looked at him hard and frowned.

She said, "Dave, I hadn't noticed this before, but I think you left his head a little thick."

Dave was a very good carver, and people never criticized his work. "Humph!" he said. "You must be mistaken. His head is perfect, except for the scrape he got on his chin yesterday."

"Maybe it was, but it's not now. This horse has a swelled head. Come take a look."

Dave grumbled as he walked over to Ambassador. But his eyes got wide and his mouth dropped open when he came around to the front of the horse. He examined Ambassador like a doctor would examine a patient. He looked in the horse's mouth, up his nose, inside his ears, and gasped. "I can't believe I carved him like that! I was so sure he was perfectly proportioned, but you're right. This horse does have a serious case of the big head!"

Dave grabbed a tool and started peeling away wood. "I'm sorry this is going to delay things, but he has to be cut down to size. I'll just take off a little around the ears. Can you come back and paint tomorrow?"

"Sure. No problem."

Sandy left and Dave got to work. He was very quiet at first. He just shaved and sanded and shaved and sanded. But after a while he started talking again and he said very nice things to Ambassador. Ambassador liked hearing compliments. It felt good to be glorious and splendid.

That night, long after Dave had gone home, Ambassador continued to think about all the nice things he'd said.

I love being important! he thought.

The next morning when Ambassador woke up, Dave and Sandy were standing in front of him. Dave was tapping his foot and Sandy was shaking her head from side to side.

Dave grumbled. "Do you think the wood might be swollen because of the humidity?"

Sandy shrugged. "That's possible, I guess. It *has* been raining a lot. None of the other horses got swelled heads, though."

Other horses? Ambassador thought. *Who cares about other horses? I'm the important one – the special one – the beautiful one.*

"What do you think I should do?" Dave asked.

"I guess you'll just have to keep working on him. His head is still too big, and now that I look closer, I think maybe his chest is a little puffed up, too."

"This can't be happening!" Dave exclaimed. "He was perfect!"

Sandy patted Dave gently on the shoulder. "You're a very good carver, but no one's perfect. Why don't you have another go at it?"

And that's the way it went. Every day Dave came by and cut Ambassador down to size, and by the next morning Ambassador's head was as swollen as if someone had blown up a balloon inside of it.

Being beautiful and special and important was great fun, and Ambassador enjoyed the attention.

He thought his little game with Dave would go on forever. But then one morning when he woke up he found himself standing all alone in a very dark closet. For days no one came around to tell him how pretty he was. He didn't even get to see Dave. Ambassador was lonely. There was no one to talk to and nothing to do. He got very bored and the weight of his big head was starting to give him a terrible pain in the neck.

So one morning when two strange men came and lifted him out of the closet Ambassador was excited. Was he finally going to a party? Was he going to lead a parade? Was he getting ready to meet some important people?

One of the men grunted and said, "Let's set him down here. Careful now. We're going to have to lean him up against this wall."

"He can't stand up?"

"Not on his own. He's off balance because of the swelled head and puffed up chest."

"Isn't that a shame! All that hard work gone to waste. What are they going to do with him?"

"Beats me. I don't think he's good for much of anything now. I suppose someone will come around later and haul him off."

"Will they carve another ambassador horse?"

"I don't know. But they sure couldn't take this fat-head out to represent the Carousel."

Ambassador gulped. He didn't know a lot, but he knew those men were talking about him. And those weren't compliments! This didn't feel good at all.

He looked around. He was someplace unfamiliar. He would have been scared if it weren't for the strange but wonderful new sounds he was hearing. Ambassador tried to see where the brilliant notes, blaring horns, and pounding drums were coming from, but he couldn't lift his head high enough to see the band organ. He could only lift his eyes.

When he did, he saw something amazing. Right there in front of him were rows and rows of fabulous horses all going around in a big circle. There were white ones and black ones, pintos and palominos. Some were running; some were standing. There were horses with armor and horses with sparkling jewels. There were wagons, shields, hundreds of ribbons, and thousands of twinkling lights.

And there were children!

The sight of them took Ambassador's breath away. Children were riding on the backs of those beautiful horses, their eyes sparkling with the wonder of it all.

Oh, how he wished his knees would bend. If he could only walk, he'd jump up on the Carousel and join them. He wanted to be a part of this glorious, splendid thing.

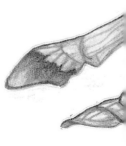

As the Carousel turned he caught a glimpse of a goofy looking horse in one of the mirrors. He started to laugh, but then he saw that the horse had carvings on two sides. There was a carousel on one side and tools on the other.

Ambassador gulped. *That can't be me! That can't be me! Oh, please, please, please; don't let THAT be me!*

But it *was* him, and he knew it. All of the other horses were on the Carousel, and each one of them was beautiful. Ambassador was the horse with the humongous, swollen, fat head. And not only that . . . he was totally naked! He wasn't wearing one dab of paint.

Ambassador was horrified. He tried to run away and hide. But his knees were locked. They wouldn't budge. He had no choice but to stand right out there in the open with his big fat head and his pale wooden body for the entire world to see. He thought he was about as low as a horse could get until people started pointing and laughing. When he realized they were laughing at him, he suspected he'd done something very, very wrong. He just didn't know what.

Later that day a little girl and her mother stopped and looked at Ambassador on their way to buy tickets to ride. "What happened to him, Mama?" the little girl asked.

"No one knows for sure. He was supposed to be the ambassador for the Carousel. They meant for him to travel around the state to represent all of the beautiful horses carved and painted by the volunteers."

"What went wrong?"

"No one knows, honey, but he sure turned out to be a disappointment. Come on, now. Let's go ride a pretty one." The woman took her daughter by the hand and they walked away.

Ambassador felt sick in his tummy. *What a fool I've been! I thought I was so important! I thought it was all about me! But it never was! It was about the entire carousel! It was about the carvers and the sanders and the painters and all of the other horses. I was only IMPORTANT because of the job I was supposed to do, and now I've blown it! They're going to get rid of me! And who could blame them? It's just what I deserve.*

He hung his big, fat head in shame.

He thought and he thought, trying to figure a way out of this mess. If he could only talk! He'd tell the other horses how sorry he was for thinking he was so important. If he could just tell the carvers and painters how much he admired them for all the work they had done, maybe they'd give him another chance. But there was nothing he could do. He couldn't walk and he couldn't talk, so he just stood there feeling sad and sorry.

The change that came over Ambassador was gradual. Some time around noon he realized he didn't need to lean against the wall for balance any more. A few hours after that he discovered he could actually lift his head and look around, and by the end of the day he felt positively light-headed.

Could it be? He was almost afraid to hope, but he had to look. He lifted his eyes to the mirror.

HALLELUJAH!

His fat head had shrunk back to a normal size! He looked at himself and then at all of the other carousel horses and his heart leapt with joy.

He silently pleaded, *Please, please, please, give me one more chance. I'll work hard every day and I'll make all of you proud.*

It took a while for Dave to trust the wood in Ambassador's head again. But when the swelling had been gone for two full weeks, he finally asked Sandy to start painting.

Ambassador was so happy to not be naked any more, and he was so grateful that he was going to get to do the job he'd been carved to do, that he became the hardest working horse ever.

Now he travels from place to place all around Oregon. Sometimes he rides for miles and miles in his trailer, standing still for hours at a time while people crowd around him saying things like, "He is so special! So beautiful! So important!"

Ambassador just smiles humbly and lets it all go in one ear and out the other. Because once he understood what it really meant to be an ambassador, he never, ever again allowed flattery or compliments to go to his head.

The End

Goldie

Written and Illustrated by
Janee Hughes

It had been a long, hard day and Goldie was very tired, but her rider kept urging her onward, despite fatigue, hunger, and the swift approach of darkness. Long shadows cast by tall hemlocks and firs made it difficult for the young horse to find the best footing over the rocks and windfalls. Branches with prickly needles brushed against her golden sorrel coat, now caked with sweat and dust. In a weary voice, her rider was still calling, "Mindy! Mindy!"

Goldie's usual routine had been disrupted before dawn. She awoke from a sound sleep when her master, Van, arrived two hours early with her breakfast of hay and grain. Usually that meant a trip in the horse trailer, and sure enough, she had hardly finished eating when Van returned with a halter and blanket. But she didn't get the thorough brushing she expected on these occasions. And no one washed her snowy white socks or combed out her creamy mane. Instead, Van quickly buckled on the blanket and led her out to the trailer. Bright stars shone in the dark summer sky.

After a long ride, the trailer finally came to a stop. Goldie heard Van's footsteps and then the release of the latch on the tailgate. She backed out onto a gravel parking lot, but to her surprise, there were no buildings nearby. The area was completely surrounded by tall trees. The air was cold and crisp, and she could still see some stars in the brightening sky. The strange new sights and sounds were a bit scary, and she blew through her nose and pranced at the end of her halter rope.

As Van spoke soothing words and tied her to the trailer, Goldie noticed the familiar smells of other horses. Ah! That was more like it. She looked around and recognized some of them, also tied to trailers. People in heavy jackets stood in a group, and bright lights flashed from two vehicles.

Soon Van removed Goldie's blanket and put on her saddle. But that was another strange thing. Where was her beautiful corona saddle pad, and where were her silver studded bridle and breast collar? She always wore them when she joined other horses for exhibitions and parades.

Van led her to a group of other horses and their riders. Everyone listened to a man as he talked and pointed to a large piece of paper. Goldie wished she could understand better. She turned to a bay mare near her and asked, "What's going on? Why are we out here in the middle of nowhere?"

"I'm afraid I don't know," she replied. "But I think we're in for some work. Haven't you ever been on a ride like this?"

"No," Goldie said. "I'm a posse horse. I perform in large buildings and prance down city streets with other horses dressed up just like me. I've never been to a place like this!"

The other mare tossed her mane and snorted. "Wow—you really *are* green! You think being a posse horse is about showing off, don't you? But this is the most important part of being a posse horse!"

Before Goldie could ask her to explain, the bay mare turned and walked off with her rider. Van mounted and they followed a group of other horses out of the parking lot and onto a wide trail that led under the trees.

Excited by all the new sights and sounds, Goldie arched her neck and pranced sideways down the trail. Most of the other horses walked quietly. Goldie recognized an older chestnut horse in front of her and worked her way closer. Annoyed, the chestnut switched his tail and pinned back his ears.

"Don't run over me, young lady! You better save some of that energy. You're going to need it before the day is over!"

"What are we doing here, anyway?" Goldie asked. "We're posse horses. We put on drill demonstrations and lead parades! There should be crowds of people here to watch us. I don't understand."

"Posse horses have a lot more important things to do than provide entertainment," the chestnut replied. "We're here to search for a lost person. People don't have very good instincts when they get out in the woods. It may seem hard to believe, but they can't tell which way is home, like we can, so sometimes we have to go look for them."

"Huh! Sounds pretty stupid to me! I'd much rather be wearing my fancy tack and prancing through town in the Governor's Guard!"

The trail turned up a hill, and Goldie soon settled into a steady walk, breathing hard as she carried her rider up the steep incline. Then, as the trail flattened out, the horses began to separate and go in different directions. Soon she was alone. Alarmed, she called out to the other horses and began prancing again. Van urged her on through the trees, and soon she could no longer hear the other horses. She felt frightened, alone in this unfamiliar place. She tossed her head and pulled on the bit, trying to turn back to the trailer. "Goldie, cut that out and settle down!" Van scolded. Goldie quickly obeyed, regretting that she had been naughty.

Throughout the long day, Goldie walked through the woods, sometimes on rocky ground and other times on soft grass and fir needles. She climbed up hills and down canyons and stream beds. All of it seemed so pointless. Sometimes they were headed toward the trailer and she walked on eagerly, but then Van would turn her away again. And every few minutes he yelled out, "Mindy, Mindy," as if expecting someone to answer.

Gradually Goldie relaxed as she became accustomed to her new surroundings. She began to look forward to seeing what was beyond the next huge tree or rocky outcropping. Once, they rested beside a small stream. Goldie drank the clear sweet water and nibbled grass while Van sat on a log and ate a sandwich. The afternoon was warm with the sun high in the sky. It was very peaceful and quiet.

But now, as evening approached, Goldie began to wish for some rest in her comfortable box stall, with a manger full of hay. She was getting very tired. As the shadows grew longer, the thin air grew colder. She noticed Van putting on his jacket. She also noticed that his calls were getting farther apart and his voice sounded tired.

Suddenly an unexpected smell drifted past her nostrils. It was faint, but unmistakable—human, and mixed with it, blood. She stopped and turned her head into the breeze. Yes, there it was again. She nickered. Van tried to turn her away, but she held her ground. She hated to disobey, but she sensed that this was important. Van dismounted, and standing beside Goldie's head, asked, "What is it, girl?" Goldie moved toward the thicket in front of her. Van parted the low branches and stepped out of sight. Soon he emerged, carrying a child.

The little girl was limp in the man's arms. She was missing a shoe and her clothes were torn. Her face was scratched and streaked with a mixture of dirt, dried blood and tears. Her eyes were closed and she was shivering, but she began to stir and whimper. Van removed his jacket and gently wrapped her in it. "It's OK, Mindy," he said soothingly. "You're safe now."

Mindy slowly opened her eyes. In a weak voice she said, "I'm so tired. I walked and walked but I couldn't find Mommy."

"I'll put you on this pretty horse and we'll take you to your mommy right away."

Goldie stood quietly while Van lifted the child and they both settled onto her back. She began to understand that she had done something very important today, something much more important than prancing in a parade. She forgot about her fatigue as she headed back to the trailer. This time Van didn't turn her away. She stepped carefully over rocks and through brush. By the time they reached the trail, night had fallen; but her instincts and a tiny sliver of moon helped her find the way.

Finally they reached the parking lot and the trailers. Many people gathered around as they walked out of the woods, some of them leading horses. As they made their way through the crowd, Goldie noticed the chestnut she had talked to that morning. He perked up his ears and softly nickered, "Well, what do you know!"

A woman came running, crying, "Mindy! Oh, my baby! You found her!" As Van handed Mindy down from the saddle, the woman hugged her and sobbed, "Oh, thank you, sir! Thank you!"

"It's Goldie here you should be thanking," Van replied. "She's the one who found her."

Van dismounted stiffly. A man walked up to him, shook his hand, and said, "We can't thank you and your horse enough. She must be a fine animal."

"That she is!" her master replied, giving Goldie an affectionate pat. "If it hadn't been for Goldie, poor little Mindy would still be out there."

The little girl turned in her mother's arms, touched Goldie's soft nose, and said, "Thank you, Goldie."

Now Goldie understood—*this* was the most important part of being a posse horse!

Goldie now carries children on Salem's Riverfront Carousel. Wearing her silver mounted saddle, bridle, and breast collar, and her beautiful corona saddle pad, she represents the wonderful posse horses who give so much for the people they serve.

The End

Snickerdoodle

Written by
Chris Patterson

Illustration by
Kathy Haney

Tsk, Tsk

Snickerdoodle snickered
As she doodled in her stall.
She dipped her tail in purple paint
And slapped it on the wall.
Did she get caught?
Of course!
Oh, what a naughty horse!

Magic

Written and Illustrated by
Sandy Walker

"I don't want to go ANY FURTHER!!" Anna said, stomping her foot. "I hate this dusty old trail. I miss Magic, and I want to go HOME!"

"Stop it, Anna," her mama scolded. "You know we couldn't bring along your old horse. He would never have made the trip. We're all tired and grouchy today, but look up ahead. Those are the Cascade Mountains. Our new home is not so far away now."

Her parents had said traveling the Oregon Trail would be an adventure. Some adventure! Every day she got up early, helped her mama pack the bedding and breakfast dishes into the wagon, and then she walked and walked until evening. She walked until her feet ached. She walked along that dusty trail with only Brownie the cow to talk to day after day. She walked in the rain and in the hot sun. Bump, bump, bump, the wagon rolled along.

Anna was tired. Her feet hurt. Her lips were chapped, and she was lonely. If they had just let her bring Magic, it might have been better. She and Magic used to roam the fields back home. She would tell the white horse secrets, and it seemed he understood. But her parents said Magic was too old to make the trip, so they left him in the care of a neighbor. And now her heart ached whenever she thought of him.

After dinner that evening, Anna's mama gave her a basin of water, told her to wash up, and sent her off to bed before it was fully dark. "Tomorrow things will look better," she said. That was often Mama's advice, but it didn't make Anna feel any better.

Anna lay in her bed listening to the sounds of Mama cleaning up the dishes, feeling mad, or was it sad? She wasn't quite sure. But as she drifted off to sleep, she knew one thing for sure – she was not happy.

Sometime later, Anna sat up with a start! She heard a sound like a soft whinny nearby. The moon had come up, and the world was bathed in silver light. She crept quietly from her little bed and out into the night. A short distance away she saw the ghostlike form of a grazing horse. It was white and very like her own horse, Magic.

"Magic?" she exclaimed without thinking. The horse lifted his head and began to approach her. He looked younger and friskier than her old horse. She stood very still as he came closer. The horse whinnied softly and touched his velvet muzzle against Anna's cheek, just as Magic had done hundreds of times before.

She threw her arms around his neck. It was Magic! "How did you get here? Oh, Magic, I have missed you so! This trip has been so long and I am so tired and homesick. Thank you for coming."

Then Magic slowly began to retreat, first looking back at her, then forward, as if he were beckoning her to follow. The thought came that her parents would not like her outside like this at night, but she knew she could trust her old friend. So, she followed him through the sagebrush, up to the top of a small hill which seemed very bright in the light of the moon. Stopping at the top, he stomped his foot several times, looking down at the ground in front of him. As Anna caught up with him, she saw the glint of something shiny on the ground. She cautiously reached out and picked it up. It was a golden medallion. How curious! She looked at it more closely, turning it over in her hand. It wasn't like any coin she had seen before, as it had the image of a flying horse, of all things. "How lovely! Thank you, Magic," she said. "I will treasure it." Then she slipped the medallion in the pocket of her gown.

As she did, the strangest thing she'd ever seen began to happen right before her eyes. Magic began to change. A bump formed on his forehead and then wings erupted from his shoulders. She blinked. Was this a dream? Then she saw it…a single horn growing from his forehead, glowing with a golden inner light. She would have been frightened if it had happened to anyone but Magic.

As Anna trembled in amazement, Magic stepped toward her and kneeled down, beckoning with his head. "Climb on," he seemed to be saying. She mounted his back just as she had done many times, holding his mane in her fingers. Then slowly, quietly, but with great power, those beautiful shimmering wings spread, and with a whoosh, Anna felt herself lifted from the ground and up, up into the night sky.

Things looked very different from above in the moonlight. It was beautiful! Over the sagebrush desert they flew until the land became great hills darkened with pine trees. She saw rivers that looked like silver ribbons strewn about and the snowy peaks of mountains. Magic flew in an arc through the sky – first toward the North Star, then west to where the sun had set. Below, to her right, a very large river came

into view. They flew along its course. A mighty mountain rose up on their left. Its peak was snow-covered and majestic.

She heard the sound first and then saw a tall crystal waterfall cascading above the river. There were more forests than Anna had ever seen in her life! The trees were dark, but the whole landscape appeared soft and mysterious in the moonlight. Soon, in the pale light, she realized they had veered away from the big river and turned down a smaller one. She could see the roofs of houses and barns. People lived here – children and families.

The forest gradually opened into a wide valley dotted with trees. It looked very lush and inviting. Could this be the Willamette Valley where her family was headed? She thought of the great ocean that she had heard was not far beyond the valley. She would see it one day. Anticipation rose in her heart, and all of her weariness and dread seemed to be blown away with the breeze as they flew. Magic headed down the valley and soon began a descent into a grassy meadow, landing on a little knoll. "My family will live here!" Anna thought, though she didn't know how she knew. "I bet Papa will build our cabin right here where we can look out and see the stream." She felt very happy!

Magic touched the ground and trotted down the hill. Stopping at a gurgling stream, he bent down to take a drink. Anna leaned over his neck to look at the moon's reflection in the water. She didn't realize it, but at that moment, the golden medallion slipped from her pocket and landed in the soft grass.

Magic and Anna wandered about the meadow a bit. Anna looked carefully, wanting to remember it all. Then as the moonlight began to fade, they rose again into the sky and began the journey back over the mountains to the wagon train. The rhythm of those wings was so peaceful; it made Anna sleepy…

The next thing Anna remembered was awakening snug under her quilt in her little wagon box bed. The birds were singing, and the morning was becoming golden. As she lay there, the dream—if that was what it was—still floated through her sleepy head. Suddenly, she sat up with a start, wide awake! She quickly put her hand in her gown pocket. The medallion was gone! Disappointment filled her. It must have been a dream. How real it had seemed! Anna quickly dressed. She had to tell her parents!

Papa was caring for the oxen. Mama already had the fire going, heating the pot of porridge. As Anna ran from the wagon, Mama was calling, "Papa, breakfast!" As they sat down to share their breakfast, Mama said, "Anna, you look so bright and cheerful today."

"I had the most amazing dream!" Anna blurted out.

Papa raised his hand to silence her so he could ask God's blessing on their food and journey as he did each day. "And please send us a helper to watch over and guide us as we travel over these mountains. Amen."

This was Anna's opportunity. "Papa, I saw God's helper last night! He is my own Magic. He's come to lead us to our new home." She told her wonderful dream in great detail, including the part about the beautiful green valley.

"Now that was one big dream for my little girl!" Papa chuckled, "but I wasn't exactly expecting a flying horse for a helper!"

Anna felt a little embarrassed. She thought Papa was laughing at her. But the truth was, the unusual dream stuck in all their hearts, and they did think of it as they crossed the mountains.

Several weeks later, they came to the end of that long, dusty trail. What a trip it had been! Mama and Anna waited in Oregon City, so thankful to rest and to be in a bustling town again. Papa explored the land further south, looking for the best place to homestead.

He laid claim to a small farm. When Anna first saw the place, it reminded her of the dream, but she kept the thought to herself. Papa built a small cabin before winter, with a window that looked down toward the stream. The neighbors helped each other that winter; and though they weren't able to plant crops until spring, there were fish and deer, berries and nuts, and the promise of spring. With all there was to do, Anna nearly forgot her dream.

When Christmas came that year, of course there wasn't much with which to celebrate, but Mama made it special in little ways—a lovely meal of venison stew and bread pudding, some boughs of cedar and fir around the room. And on Christmas Eve they sat down before the crackling fire together. Then Mama handed Anna a small package wrapped in brown paper tied with a piece of red yarn. "Oh, what could it possibly be?" She was so excited!

"Open it," Papa said, with a twinkle in his eye. And so she did. Papa had carved something special for her from a small piece of light colored cedar wood. It was Magic, her horse, except he had wings and a beautiful horn on his forehead—just like in her dream!

Anna gave her parents the small gifts she had made for them as well—a simple cross-stitch to Mama, a handkerchief to Papa. Then, sitting before the fire, they spoke of all they were grateful for and reminisced about family back home and their long trip west. "This has certainly been the most difficult year of our lives," Mama said, "one we won't soon forget."

"Yes, but we've made it safely. We have a fine new home, friends, food, and much to be thankful for," Papa replied.

"I'm glad we came, too," added Anna.

When the fire burned low, Papa and Anna went outside to get another log or two. It was a frosty, clear night with many stars and a half-moon. Their boots crunched the frozen grass as they walked a short way down the path. The stream below gurgled and shone silver in the pale light. As Papa bent to lift a log from the pile, his eye caught the glint of something hidden in the grass. He reached to uncover it

and picked up what appeared to be a large golden coin. He held it up to catch the moonlight so he could see it better. "Papa, look!" Anna cried out, "It's the coin Magic gave me! It has the golden horse with the wings!"

Papa just stood there for a long time, looking at the medallion, then at his little girl, with wonder in his heart. Then he hugged her close to his side and they walked home together.

The End

Carousel Dreams

Words & Music by
Nancy M. Hadley

Musical Arrangement by
Ruth LaFreniere

Illustration by
Michelle Jondrow Schultz

This song is dedicated to the Salem Riverfront Carousel project, the horse Rosinante, (representing the brave-hearted nag of the legendary Don Quixote) and to all those who dare to "dream impossible dreams!" It was performed on opening day of the Carousel in June, 2001.

Carousel Dreams

Chorus:

If you dream the impossi-ble, there's al-ways a way! Although the ring of brass seems

so far a-way Wind mills or carousels, just follow the gleam, for all things are possible

if you can dream. 1. A dream, that was born as the ti-ni-est seed gave

way to a vision of fill-ing a need; A park on the riverfront pro-

vi-ded the space for a neighborhood carousel to be put in-to place

VERSES:

2. It took many people who truly believed,
   That a project this *big* could be somehow achieved;
   There were those who said, "No! This plan never will fly!"
   But others who just would not let this dream die! CHORUS

3. Then from all around town there began to appear,
   Many folks who were willing to just volunteer;
   To work and to help any way that they could,
   From designing and drawing to carving the wood.

4. The dream had caught fire; it was easy to see
   This Riverfront Carousel just had to be!
   The horses were fashioned; no two were the same!
   Each one was 'adopted' and given a name! CHORUS

5. And though carousel horses were mostly the rule,
   There were ponies, a zebra, and one 'winking' mule!
   And a mystical unicorn, with wings, that could fly!
   And magically carry each child through the sky

6. The children of Salem were eager to ride,
   Their anticipation they just could not hide;
   When the carousel opened, each one was so thrilled!
   The magic was real; the dream was fulfilled! CHORUS

Sonshine's
Second Career

Written and Illustrated by
Janee Hughes

It was the worst day of my life! I thought we were going to another horse show. Sarah gave me a bath and brushed my mane and tail 'til they were silky soft. She led me into the trailer, and the next thing I knew, we were at a strange farm, and Sarah was hugging me and crying.

"Good-bye, Sonshine," she sobbed, "I know you'll be very happy here. I'll be away at college a long time, and you need children to love you. I'll miss you a lot, but I promise to come back and visit you." Then she handed my lead rope over to a strange man, got in the truck, and drove away.

I just couldn't believe it! We'd been together ever since I could remember. What about all the trail rides and shows and all the ribbons and trophies we won? Didn't that mean anything?

Sarah was leaving me! It hurt deep down inside. The stranger pulled at my halter rope, but I refused to move 'til the trailer was out of sight. Then I hung my head and followed him into a big barn where he put me in a stall.

The stall was clean and there was some sweet-smelling alfalfa hay, but I wasn't interested in eating. As I hung my head over the door, the gray mare in the next stall introduced herself.

"Hello, I'm Lucy. You must be Sonshine. I heard you were coming." She sounded as old as she looked—she must have been at *least* twenty.

"Why did everyone know about this except me? What kind of place is this, anyway?"

"It's called 'Therapy Ranch.' Children with disabilities come here to learn to ride. They need gentle, dependable horses. For most of us, it's a second career."

"You mean I'm being turned out to pasture? I'm not *that* old!"

"Not all the horses here are old, just experienced. And it's really not so bad—in fact, it can be very rewarding. I'm sure the children are going to love you with your flashy paint coat."

"Huh!' I said, and turned back into my stall. I spent the rest of the evening and all night feeling blue and hoping that Sarah would come back for me.

The next morning I was pretty hungry and ate a bit of hay. People came in the barn and groomed and saddled the other horses. I had to admit, it seemed a happy, friendly place. But then the horses were led away, and I was left all alone. I felt even sadder than before.

After a couple of hours, the horses returned with their handlers. "I have some news for you, Sonshine," Lucy said, "I heard that the head trainer, Bill, is going to take you out and show you the farm before the afternoon session."

"I guess that's better than standing around here all day," I grumbled.

Soon a tall, dark man approached my door. He spoke my name softly and stroked my face. I could tell he understood the way I felt. I liked this Bill.

Bill was an expert with brushes, and I enjoyed the relaxing massage as he groomed my whole body. Then he saddled me and led me outside, across the yard, and into another building. It was a large indoor arena, and it reminded me of horse shows with Sarah. With an aching heart, I nickered for her. Bill patted my neck and mounted. His weight settled gently into the saddle, and I knew instantly that he was an expert rider. I easily understood the commands he communicated with his seat and legs, and I obeyed confidently. He rode me around the arena several times and then out another door into the sunlight.

Suddenly I saw a bright flash behind me, and at the same instant something crashed painfully into my right hind leg. I jumped forward and wheeled around to face my attacker. It was a shiny metal chair with big wheels attached. I snorted and backed away as it came to a stop against the building.

"Whoa, Sonshine!" said Bill. "Sorry about that. Someone forgot to set the brake on that wheelchair. Easy, now." Maybe it was a chair to him, but it looked like a vicious predator to me!

Bill got off and looked at my leg. I knew it was just a scratch. Then he tried to lead me towards the horrible chair. I couldn't see any point in getting closer to that cold, hard steel monster. It had already attacked me once! So I refused and backed up.

"You're going to have to get used to this, Sonshine, if you're going to be a therapy horse," Bill said. I had no intention of getting used to it, *or* of becoming a therapy horse! He got back on and rode me around a field and through some trees. I began to relax. But going back to the barn, I shied away from the chair again.

That afternoon, the other horses all left again, while I stayed in my stall. Lucy explained that they worked with two groups of children each day. When they came back, they were all turned loose in a field. And this time I went, too. The freedom of the open air made some of the horses frisky and playful. Others enjoyed the sweet grass. But I ran down to the end of the fence where I had last seen my trailer. I stayed there 'til the grooms came to take us in for the night.

For the next few days, the routine was the same. The other horses went out for the morning and afternoon sessions. Bill took me out between classes. He kept trying to get me close to the wheelchair, but I was still afraid of another attack.

"You are a fine horse, Sonshine," Bill said, "except when it comes to that blasted wheelchair! Unfortunately, that's pretty important in your new job! I hope we don't have to find another home for you."

Oh no! I didn't know it was possible to flunk out of an old horse home! Did that mean I'd have to go somewhere else, and not back to Sarah? I was devastated!

During our turn-out time late that afternoon, I was looking down the road, longing to see Sarah, when a van drove in the gate. I watched, curious, as it stopped near me and two people got out. "Oh, look, Bruce," the lady said, "What a beautiful horse!"

The man walked around the van and replied, "He sure is. I wonder if Joshua will get to ride that one."

The lady walked up and stroked my nose, but then I saw the man pulling a wheelchair out of the van. I snorted and backed up, ready to turn and flee.

"What's wrong ?" the lady said.

Bruce lifted a boy from the back of the van and placed him in the chair. The boy's thin legs dangled, motionless. Then Bruce pushed the chair toward me, the wheels flashing in the sun.

Seeing that thing coming towards me, I snorted again and I almost fled. But then I noticed something else. The boy in the chair was looking at me, with a huge smile and laughing eyes. His face beamed with happiness.

This boy was full of life and joy, despite his handicap. He looked at me the same way Sarah had when we first met. And that was enough. I no longer noticed the wheelchair, only the boy seated in it. Bruce pushed the chair close to the fence, and I lowered my head to Joshua's outstretched hand.

"Hi, there, Bruce and Gloria," Bill said, stepping up to the newcomers. "I see you've already met Sonshine. Looks like he's taken a liking to Joshua already."

Bill slipped a halter on me and led me out the gate, closer to Joshua.

They all talked, and before long, Bill saddled me and led me to the arena. There, Joshua was gently placed in the saddle and strapped on. With Bill leading me, and Bruce and Gloria steadying Joshua, I walked slowly around the arena. The warm glow of Joshua's joy flowed into me. I could give him what he didn't have—the ability to move on real legs.

Bill told Gloria and Bruce, "I think this is going to be a good match. Learning to ride gives kids like Joshua a new sense of freedom and independence. Their self-esteem grows when they find they can control a horse, and they show marked improvement in strength and coordination."

"It's a wonderful program!" Gloria exclaimed. "I've never seen Joshua happier!"

"By the way," Bill said, "Sonshine is a pretty special horse. His paint markings include the dark coloring over his ears and poll, called a medicine hat. The Native Americans believed that the rider of such a horse would always be protected. I think we can count on Joshua being safe on Sonshine."

Then he patted my neck. "Sonshine, when Sarah comes to visit next week, she will be very proud of you!"

It was the best day of my life! I knew now that I was going to like my second career.

Sonshine is now enjoying his third career, as a carousel horse on Salem's Riverfront Carousel. He wears his fine Indian trappings as he proudly carries delighted children.

The End

*S*alem's *Riverfront Carousel* began as the dream of one woman, Hazel Patton, who inspired an entire community to create a work of art that will stand as a symbol of volunteerism and cooperation for generations to come.

It took five years and hundreds of volunteers to hand-carve and paint 42 horses and raise the $1.2 million dollars needed to construct an 11,000 square foot building that is now home to the Carousel in Salem's Riverfront Park.

Shortly after the carving began in 1996, a group of volunteer writers and illustrators with varied backgrounds and interests came together with the intention of chronicling the creation of the project.

Knowing how carousels are apt to inspire whimsy and flights of fancy, no one was surprised when the horses began to tickle the edges of our imaginations and encourage us to tell stories about courage, leadership, friendship, loyalty, and love.

Every Pony Has a Tale is the fifth children's book written and illustrated by members of Carousel Storytellers, Ink. Not every person in the group had her story or artwork included in this book. However, each one has made a tremendous contribution, because just like the Carousel itself, every story became richer and better through collaboration, reflection, and teamwork.

We hope you'll enjoy the book!

*Kathy Connor • Cheryl Degner • Janelle Graham • Nancy M. Hadley
Kathy Haney • Kathleen S. Hoth • Billy Houghton • Jodee Howard
Janee Hughes • Damaris Koontz • Christina Patterson
Elaine K. Sanchez • Sandy Walker • Kimber Williams*